Contents

BURN OUT

Robert SWINDELLS

Barrington Stoke

First published in 2007 in Great Britain by
Barrington Stoke Ltd
18 Walker Street, Edinburgh, EH3 7LP

www.barringtonstoke.co.uk

This edition first published 2014

ISBN: 978-1-78112-346-1

Printed in China by Leo

Chapter 1
One Thing I Can Do

I'm Josh Linfoot and I'm nothing. No one. Do you know how that feels? I mean, I was here first, before my sister, but that doesn't count. No. What counts is being brainy and doing well at school.

My sister's brainy. Beth. She does well at school. Mum and Dad love her. They don't give a stuff about me. It's always been like that, since the day she was born. Beth this. Beth that. See what Beth can do.

But there's one thing I can do really well. Really well. I can start fires.

I'm in Nick Mitchell's gang. His brother, Danny, is in my class. He got me into it.

It's Friday, afternoon break. Danny and me are talking.

"Saturday tomorrow and there's nothing doing," I say. "It's a bit boring."

"I'm never bored," Danny replies.

"How come?" I say.

Danny grins. "Fires. We start fires. It's great."

I stare at him. "Fires," I say. "What sort of fires?"

"All sorts," he says. "Bins, cars, sheds. Schools, sometimes."

"Schools?" He's having a laugh. He must be.

Danny nods. "Oh yeah. Remember when Colton High went up, a few years back?"

My turn to nod. "Course. It was on the news, wasn't it? Million quid damage. Don't tell me you ...?"

"Yeah – well, not me, I was only 12. It was my brother and his mates."

I stare at him. "Your brother burned Colton High?"

"Yeah, and they never got him, did they? Never will. He's too smart." He looks at me. "Why don't you come with us? It'll be something to do."

"W– when?"

"Tomorrow, if you like."

"You're doing one tomorrow?" It doesn't sound real.

"We'll be doing *something*."

"What about your brother?" I ask. "Won't he mind me turning up?"

Danny grins. "No, he won't mind. If I say you're a mate of mine. You are a mate of mine, aren't you, Josh?"

I smile, but my heart's booting me in the ribs. "Course I am, Danny."

"Three o'clock then, bus shelter by the ice rink."

I'm in a daze the rest of the afternoon. And all night. Nick Mitchell's 19. He does what he likes. Tom Dolton's in his gang, and Ishan Dass. They're hard, those guys. You don't stare at them. I can't believe they're going to let someone like me tag along.

Turns out they aren't keen at all. When I get there, it's just Danny and Nick in the shelter. The others are late.

I grin. "Hi Nick," I say, trying to sound calm.

He eyeballs me. "Listen kid," he says. "You're here because this runt ..." He smacks Danny across the back of the head, hard. "... this runt blabbed to you about gang stuff."

I look at Danny. He's trying not to cry. Nick grabs his hood, jerks him up, and starts smacking him again. "We never [smack] never [smack] never [smack] blab about the gang to anyone, not even to make ourselves feel big." He shakes his little brother. "Feel big, do you, runt?"

"N– no Nick." Danny's crying now. I don't want to look at him. It's my fault he's in trouble.

"Look," I croak, "I'll just go, all right? I didn't mean to cause –"

Nick shakes his head. "You're going nowhere – you know too much. I've got a little job ready for you, and when you've done it you'll be one of us. Which means ..." He grins. "... if we go down, you go down."

The others show up just then. Bobby Robinson, Tom Dolton, Ishan Dass and Tony Parsons. Nick tells them my name and says I'll be around from now on. He doesn't tell me their names – no need. Everyone in our town knows who they are. Knows them and fears them. Being in that bus shelter with them feels like being a tadpole in a pond of piranhas.

Chapter 2
Baby Seat

There's a 4x4 standing on waste ground where the steelworks used to be. It's a silver Marauder.

"There you go, kid," says Nick. "All yours."

I look at him. "Whose is it?" I ask.

"I told you," he murmurs. "Yours. Light it up."

"I ... haven't got a light."

The others snigger, except Danny. He's still not looking at me. Nick fishes in his pocket, hands me a lighter. "Go on."

I walk towards the 4x4. It's nearly new. No way did the owner park it here. The others must have nicked it earlier, that's why they were late. I'm shaking. My legs have gone weak. I can feel the gang's eyes on me. This is a test, to find out if I'm good enough to be a member.

I don't want to do it. They can't force me. But they'll beat me up. They might even dump me in the Marauder and set it on fire. I shiver and go up to the driver's door.

It isn't locked. The door swings open. I force myself inside. One of the back seats is fitted with a baby seat. Beside the baby seat is a box of tissues. I grab the box, pull out all the tissues and dump them on the baby seat. I tear the box in two and lay it on top. Then I flick the lighter and touch the flame to the tissues.

I'm really, really scared, but it's an amazing feeling, watching that little flame grow. In seconds the back of the baby seat is alight. Plastic foam starts to melt and trickle down. Thick black smoke pours out.

I'm kneeling on the driver's seat. I'm looking at what I've done. I'm just watching, watching ...

A voice starts yelling. It's Nick. "Get out, you idiot!" he roars. "D'you want to go up with it or what?"

I turn and jump out of the car. The fire's only been going for seconds, but the heat is terrific. Unbelievable. I leave it behind and run to where I can watch. I'm coughing from the smoke. My eyes are watering. I rub them. All I want is to watch.

Danny was right. It is great. The Marauder is a boiling, roaring furnace – like the steelworks all over again. As I watch there's an explosion – *crrrump!* I feel the blast. A fireball like an H-bomb rolls up through the smoke. 'I did this,' I think. 'Me, Loser Linfoot. Not a loser now, eh?'

People are beginning to notice the fire. The motorway flyover's not far off. Cars are stopping. Drivers, like little dolls up there, are pointing.

Nick sees them. "Right," he snaps. "Time to split. Hurry up, kid."

We scatter. I head for the little streets behind the waste ground. A siren wails. When I stop for a breather, it's just me and Danny.

I grin and wipe the sweat off my face with my sleeve. "That was awesome," I gasp. "The way it went up, in seconds."

Danny nods. He leans on a wall. "Now you know why I'm never bored."

"Sure do. What about tomorrow?" I ask.

He laughs. "Nothing tomorrow. Gang's got other stuff to see to. Business. Nick doesn't like us kids around then. I'll see you at school, Monday."

We split up. I'm dying to go back, watch the firemen tackle the blaze. *My* blaze. But I don't. I go home.

"You smell funny," says Beth, the second I walk in. Nine years old, eyes like a hawk, nose like a sniffer dog. Nothing gets by Beth.

"Bonfire," I grunt, "up the allotments."

I go to my room and change my clothes before Mum smells me too. After tea I watch the local news, but there's nothing about the fire. Shame.

But the story's not over. I wake up sweating and shaking in the middle of the night. I've had a dream about the baby seat. A nightmare. I was watching the flames catch hold when something moved. I saw there was a baby in the car seat. It sat kicking like they do and waving its arms about, too young to know what was happening. It kept reaching for the flames. I started to run back towards the car. I was crying out, "I didn't know". But I was beaten back by the heat. The baby seat was melting and tipping to one side. The baby started to cry now and stretched chubby arms towards me. I tried, but I couldn't get near. I saw the baby's soft skin begin to blister and smoke. It was so horrible, so real, I had to wake up to escape.

It was a warning, that nightmare, but I didn't know. Didn't know there are nightmares you can't escape, 'cos you're not asleep.

Chapter 3

Dope

I'm excited when I walk into school on Monday morning. I'm a new Josh Linfoot now. I'm sure people will know by the way I look. 'There goes Josh,' they'll whisper. 'Josh the firestarter – one of Nick Mitchell's gang.'

It doesn't happen, of course. Nothing happens, except Danny asks if I'm all right.

"Fine," I tell him. I hope he'll say something about next Saturday, but he nods and walks off. Still getting grief from big brother, I expect.

It turns out I won't have to wait till Saturday. On Tuesday morning Danny comes up to me and says, "Tonight, half six, allotment gates."

I corner him at lunchtime. I ask, "What is it tonight?"

"Shed job," he says. "Shed and greenhouse."

"Whose?" My dad's got an allotment. I hope we aren't going after his shed.

"Wait and see," he says. "Bring a lighter this time."

There's no need to tell me – I always carry a lighter now, sort of like a badge. To show I'm a member.

It's drizzling at half six. Getting dark. There'll be no gardeners about on this nasty March evening. Nick opens the gate and we troop along the path. "This is the one," he says.

There's a rickety gate in the hedge. Ishan Dass kicks it down and we trample on it as we go into the allotment.

It's a good shed. It has thick pine boards, newish, stained with creosote paint. It stands on a brick base. There's a window in the side and a little one in the door. The door's padlocked.

"Get the lock," says Nick, and Tony Parsons moves towards it. The rest of us turn to the greenhouse.

It's newish, like the shed. Big, too. "Room for lots of tomatoes to grow in here," I say.

"Tomatoes!" Nick spits the word. "Heated unit, that. You can grow dope in there. And sell it on. Make a nice load of money. That's what this guy was going to do for me, but he wimped out." Nick picks up a stone. "The greenhouse won't burn. We'll smash the glass," he says.

We smash the glass with stones, boots and a spade from the shed. I get nervous – it makes so much noise. But no one comes. Who'd be daft enough to bother? It's dark and there are seven of us.

I want to light the shed, but Ishan gets the job. He's found a can of paraffin. Perfect. We watch him splash it everywhere, inside and out. Then he soaks a rag in it, lights it, and chucks it into the shed.

The shed goes up with a whoosh. There's a drum of creosote that's left from when the shed was stained. Paraffin's good, but creosote's better. When the flames reach it we all cheer. The explosion blows out a side of the shed. Sparks whirl on the damp air. What's left of the shed sags, crackling. Roof felt burns well, too.

Soon we hear sirens. We have to leave the fire, but we don't run off. There are plenty of shadowy places to hide. Danny and I head for the next-door allotment. There's a shed there too. An old one. We slide between that and the hedge.

"Get some stones," Danny hisses.

The firemen drive an engine along the pathway, run out the hose and start looking for a tap. Showers of stones come from the darkness, like hail. The firemen dodge about. They're cursing and swearing, putting their arms up to cover their faces. One's on his mobile.

"He's calling for backup," says Danny. "Get him."

We pelt the guy till he scuttles behind the vehicle, where he comes under attack from another direction. Why am I not scared stiff? I should be. But I'm not. There's no time to be scared. I'm pumped up, high as a kite. I want it to go on forever.

It doesn't. After a few minutes come more sirens, blue flashes, sounds of barking.

"Police dogs," cries Danny. "Come on."

We get away. Everyone runs for it. I admit I was scared when I heard those dogs, but we never saw them. I've smashed glass, watched a blaze, used living guys for target practice! All in all, it's the most excitement I've had in a long time. The most *ever*.

Who needs dope when you're totally hooked on fire?

Chapter 4
Want Locking Up

"What on earth's happened, Josh?" says Mum when I walk in. "You look as if you've been dragged through a hedge backwards."

I know I'm a mess, so I've got my excuse ready. "We were in the park, Mum. Me and Danny. Some guys chased us. We ran into the bushes to get away, but it was all mud and dead leaves."

"I don't know." Mum shakes her head. "14, and still playing kids' games. I hope you'll grow out of it one day."

"It wasn't a *game*, Mum," I protest. "The guys chasing us were muggers. They were after our phones. It's not like when you were young."

Of course, Mum's all worried then. She wants to call the police. I have a job convincing her that there's no need to do that.

There's excitement next day as well. I get in from school and Dad's home already. He's an estate agent and doesn't have fixed hours. I know by his red face that something's got him stirred up.

"Something up, Dad?" I ask.

"I'll say." He's got the local paper. He flaps it in my face. "Look at this."

I squint at the front-page photo. My heart lurches. It's the allotment we trashed last night. 'He knows,' goes a voice inside my skull. 'I'm dead.'

"Look at it," he bellows. "Where's the sense in that? Jim Pickard owned that allotment. He spent hundreds of pounds last year, putting in a new greenhouse, new shed. Just so some brainless goons can come along and destroy it all." He doesn't know, thank God.

"Those guys want locking up," Dad carries on, and then he throws the paper across the kitchen. It falls apart all over the stone tiles.

"Alan," says Mum softly. She's picking up the sheets of newspaper. "It's no use getting upset. The men who did this are miles away by now. They won't be caught, so you might as well put it out of your mind. Think about something nice, like Beth's news."

"What's Beth's news?" I ask. I don't want to hear about my sister's latest miracle, but it'll stop Dad going on about the allotment.

Mum smiles. "I'll let her tell you herself," she says. "She'll be down in a minute."

Soon the four of us are sitting round the table, eating pizza and chips. Beth's still wearing her school cardie because she wants us to see her new badge. The badge is green to match the cardie, with the words 'ZOO KEEPER' in gold. I look at her.

"Zoo keeper?" I say.

She nods. "Yes. Mr Hartley's put us in charge of all the animals. Me and Kate. He had these badges specially made."

"Mr Hartley?" I echo. "Got the hots for Mr Hartley, eh, Sis?"

"No, I don't." She's gone red.

"What you blushing for, then?" I ask.

"I'm not blushing."

Mum breaks in. She doesn't like me having a go at my sister. "Tell Josh what Mr Hartley said to you and Kate, sweetheart," Mum says.

"Oh ..." Beth looks down at her plate. She's chuffed to bits, but she's good at acting modest. "He said he was giving us a responsible job because we've proved to be mature, responsible people. He said he's known plenty of adults who weren't nearly as sensible as me and Kate. He said the animals are in the safest possible hands." She glances up, embarrassed. "That's all."

"*All?*" I snort. "Wish someone'd say something like that about *me*, even if it was only once."

I'm only saying this to be nice to her, but then something swells in my throat. A big sore lump. I jump up and run out of the room.

I lie on my bed and cry, because I realise what I said to my sister is true. Josh Linfoot, fire-starter in Nick Mitchell's gang, would swap his lighter for his sister's badge in a flash, if only it were that easy.

If only.

Chapter 5
Stock Clearance Day

"I see we made the headlines, Josh."

It's Thursday morning, just before the bell goes. Danny sounds really happy.

"What? Oh, yeah." I'm not happy. I had the baby seat nightmare again and hardly slept after.

"Nick is very pleased," says Danny. "That Pickard guy tried to make him look like an idiot and no one makes Nick look like an idiot."

"Does he know who did it?" I say. "It's a bit obvious. He knows Nick has a grudge against him. What if he tells the police?"

Danny shakes his head. "Not a chance. Nick knows where he lives, him and his family. If you can burn a shed you can burn a house. Pickard knows that."

"You mean ...?" I gulp. "Nick'd set fire to a house with people inside?"

Danny shrugs. "I dunno. I don't think so ... but Pickard won't want to take the chance." He grins. "Quit worrying, Josh. Nick knows what he's doing."

Danny doesn't say anything about Saturday. I sort of hope we won't be doing anything, but a part of me – the part that's hooked on fire – can't help but hope we might.

Dawdling home on Friday afternoon, Danny says, "Big stock clearance day at Tesco tomorrow, Josh."

I frown. "So?"

"So we're the guys to make it happen. You and me."

I shake my head. "I don't know what you're on about, Danny. Make what happen?"

He puts an arm round me and tells me. He keeps his voice low.

Midday Saturday, the seven of us are at Tesco. We all got there in different ways and at different times. We're dressed in jeans and plain hoodies – we need to make sure no one can identify us from the CCTV cameras. We grab trolleys and start shopping. It's as if we don't know one another.

I cruise up and down the aisles. I load my trolley with paint, white spirit, motor oil and rubber mats. I get candles too, and firelighters and ten boxes of matches in a carton. I'm not loading this stuff at random – it's all part of Nick's cunning plan. I don't look, but I know Danny's choosing the same stuff as me. He's stacking it in his trolley and undoing a screw top here and there without letting anyone see.

I look at my watch. 12:27. Three minutes to zero. I swing my trolley round and wheel it towards the back left corner of the store, near the hanging plastic strips over the doorway to the warehouse. I take my time. Nick says it's always best not to hurry. People in a hurry get noticed.

12:29. I take the lighter out of my pocket and have a quick look round.

No one's watching. I click and get a tiny flame. One last time-check. 12:30 on the dot. I bend over the trolley and touch the flame to the corner of a rubber mat. It catches at once, because some white spirit has dribbled onto it from a leaky cap. You've got to be really careful with flammable stuff.

I roll the trolley right in under the hanging strips and walk away. I take my time. In the back right corner, Danny's doing the same.

I'm outside when the alarm begins to wail. I turn and stand and watch, just like anyone else. Inside the store, they're telling customers to file out in an orderly manner, leaving trolleys and heavy bags behind. People are leaving all right, but it isn't orderly. There's a lot of pushing and shoving, most of all near the door. There are trolleys too, and bags. Customers are close to panic, if you ask me, and you can't blame them.

It's a big place, but the store is quickly filling with thick black smoke – the sort you get from paint and rubber. Tesco staff are running about like headless chickens. They're trying to do what they should when there's a fire – follow the fire drill. But the customers just take no notice.

And so no one sees that five of the trolleys crowding the two exits are piled high with state-of-the-art electronic stuff. The security guys should be watching the doors. But they've gone racing up to the back of the store. There are two other trolleys on fire there, and some plastic strips that are carrying flames to the ceiling. And no one will notice when those five trolleys at the front go missing. There's too much going on everywhere else.

I'd love to stay and watch, but it isn't in the plan. You can't throw stones at firemen in a great open car park. And anyway, £10,000 worth of electronics is enough fun for one day.

One big stock clearance day.

Chapter 6
Getting Out of Hand

Nick promises me and Danny £500 each for our Tesco stunt.

"You'll have to wait," he warns us. "The police'll be on the look-out for the stuff we nick. We'll sit on it for a bit, then sell it when the fuss dies down."

It turns out the wait is the least of my worries. I check the local news on Sunday. There are a few CCTV photos of us, but they're blurry and not even I can tell who's who in them. But then my stomach lurches. I see a photo-fit and it looks so like me I could use it in my passport.

It turns out a Tesco customer saw a boy with a trolley who was acting in an odd way. She got a good look at my face. I was taking so much care to avoid the cameras that I must have forgotten about the other people that were there. How stupid can you be? The police get her to do a photo-fit and she's got a good memory.

I nearly crapped my pants. I might as well march down to the police station, show them the photo-fit and give myself up.

I expect Danny to say something, but he doesn't. Nor does anyone else at school on Monday and Tuesday. Maybe they've got better things to look at online than the news.

But Wednesday is the day I'm really dreading. That's the day the local paper comes, and that's one thing my dad always reads ...

I pick the paper off the mat when I get in from school and there's the photo-fit. It's in the middle of the front page. There's no way Dad's going to miss that.

I could hide the paper, chuck it in the bin or pretend it's not come today. Or I could pack a bag and run off.

I don't do any of those things. I decide the only thing I can do is act as if nothing's wrong. I put the paper on the table, change out of my uniform and help Mum get tea ready. If someone picks up the paper and gasps, and blurts out that the photo-fit looks just like me, then I'll get all cross. I'll say they must be blind – it's nothing like me.

Well – what else can I do?

The next few hours are unreal. I peel the potatoes and put them on to boil. When she's laying the table, Beth picks up the paper. I watch her as she scans the front page. I wait for her to yell, "Hey Mum – there's a picture of Josh in the paper." It doesn't happen. She puts the paper down and goes on laying the table. I can't believe it.

Not long after that I hear the car on the drive. Dad's home. By this time I'm really tense. I can't just wait there till he picks up the paper. As he opens the kitchen door, I run upstairs. I shut myself in my room. I'll stay here till I hear him start shouting, then go down and confess. To be perfectly honest, it'll be good to get it over.

Five minutes pass. Then ten. Dad *must* have looked at the paper by now – it's always the first thing he does when he gets back on a Wednesday. Maybe he's waiting, ready to grab me when I come down. Perhaps he's already on the phone to the police.

"Josh," Mum calls up the stairs. "Tea's ready, we're waiting for you."

'I bet you are,' I think. But her voice sounds normal – no strain or anything. I hope mine sounds normal too as I reply, "OK, Mum – just coming."

They're sitting round the table. Dad gives me one of his looks as I join them. Mum says, "What were you doing up there, Josh – homework?"

"Yeah," I mumble. "Geography." Well, I can't tell the truth, can I? The paper lies folded by Dad's plate. Hasn't he looked at it yet?

He *has* looked at it. As Mum's getting the pudding, he flicks the paper with his knuckles. "Getting out of hand, all this," he says.

"What's that, Dad?" I ask.

"This." He picks up the paper and shows me the front page. I swallow hard, gazing at the photo-fit that looks just like me.

"Oh, the Tesco thing."

Dad nods grimly. "Yes, the Tesco thing, as you call it. Setting fire to the place, just so they could pinch some electronics. Hundreds of people inside. It was a miracle no one was killed."

I nod and push my food round the plate. "Yes it is."

'What about the picture?' I think. 'Can't you see it's your loser son, Dad?' But I don't say this out loud, of course.

"I bet it's the same lot who torched Jim Pickard's allotment," Dad goes on.

I don't reply straight away – I can't trust my voice. After a bit I say, "Could be, I suppose – but it's not the same sort of thing really, is it?"

Dad starts shouting then. "It's *exactly* the same, Joshua. Total lack of respect for other people's property. Not to mention putting lives at risk."

All the time that he's shouting, he's waving the newspaper about. And there's my picture in it. I can't believe no one's noticed how the photo-fit looks just like me. Not my mum, not my dad or my sister. I think it's because they never really look at me. Of course a neighbour might see that it's me, or a teacher at school. I seem to have got away with it at home. But I'm not kidding myself I'm off the hook.

Every minute I'm expecting someone's hand to land on my back and tell me I'm nicked. All day Thursday and Friday I wait for the police to walk in the classroom with the Head. They'll call me out and take me to the police station. I can't believe it when Friday afternoon crawls round at last and I'm still free.

I know why I'm feeling like this. It's my conscience. I know I'm doing bad stuff, and my conscience is what made me see myself in the photo-fit. I don't suppose the photo-fit is much like me at all. It can't be, can it, or somebody would have noticed.

I wish now I'd listened to my conscience. I wish it every time I look at my sister.

Chapter 7
Tinfoil Barbs

By the weekend, I finally start to relax. Nick doesn't have anything planned. I'm glad. It's no fun being tense all the time.

On Saturday I go with Mum, Dad and my sister to the garden centre. Yes, I *know*. Sad, but I need to relax. Dad's buying stuff for the allotment – seeds and stuff like that. Me and Beth go to the aquarium section and look at the water features, tanks, and tropical fish. We stand watching the tinfoil barbs. They're my favourite. It's restful, watching them.

"Has Mr Hartley got tinfoils?" I ask my sister.

She shakes her head. "Goldfish," she says. "And an axolotyl."

"What's an axolotyl?"

Beth grins. "It's like a giant tadpole. If you feed it too much it turns into a lizard thing – a salamander."

"So how often do you feed it?"

"Once a month," she says.

"And what does it get to eat every month?"

"A big worm."

"Ugh!" I pull a face. "Glad I'm not an axolotyl then. What about the goldfish?"

"They get fed every day. Well – every school day. They can manage over the weekend, as long as you give them plenty of food on Fridays." She smiles. "Same goes for the hamsters and gerbils and guinea pigs. Me and Kate fix extra water bottles to the cages on Friday afternoons, so they'll have enough till Monday."

I nearly puke, listening to her showing off. But I need to listen. I'm starting to get a brilliant idea.

Mum calls us away then, and we drive home. Dad's in a bad mood. He'd bumped into his friend, Jim Pickard, in the garden centre. Jim was buying a new shed to replace the one we'd torched. "£340 it's costing him," says Dad. "Pity he can't get the idiots who burned his other one to pay."

Dad seems to be watching me in the car mirror, so I nod. "Yeah. Make 'em think twice, that would," I say. How normal do I sound? Can he tell what I'm feeling inside? Tinfoil barbs should be on the National Health, for stress.

Nothing happens on Sunday. I don't go with Dad to the allotment. I bet he and his mate are hammering nails into Jim's £340 shed. They'll be saying stuff like, 'I wish we were hammering these into those bad guys.'

Fire, that's what I need. A good fire, but not one that'll get me arrested. A legal fire. And I'm lucky. Last autumn, Dad tidied our back garden. Cut back the shrubs and that. He does it every November. He calls it 'Putting the garden to bed for the winter'. He piles up the rubbish at the bottom of the garden, lets it dry out a bit, then sets fire to it. And he lets me help. It's the only bit of gardening I enjoy.

Last autumn the rubbish didn't dry out. Or maybe the neighbours always had washing hanging in the garden or something. Anyway, we didn't burn the rubbish, so it lay there all winter. It's there now.

"Dad?" I say. "Can we burn the garden rubbish?"

"That's a good idea," he says.

"Be careful not to scorch the fence," Mum says. "Fire spreads, you know."

'Tell me about it,' I think but I don't say anything.

I really want to light the fire myself, but Dad doesn't think I know much about fires. But he does let me light it in the end. I use a firelighter and shove it right in at the bottom. Dad says real gardeners use old newspapers and a few dry sticks. But a firelighter's less hassle.

It's not a bad fire. Not as good as Jim Pickard's shed, of course, but not bad. Most of the stuff's pretty damp, and there's a lot of thick smoke at first. There's plenty of spitting and crackling as well.

The flames are just getting a good hold when I see something move at the bottom of the heap. It's a toad! It must have spent the winter asleep under the rubbish. It comes crawling out, moving pretty fast for a toad. It's not hurt, just surprised and a bit scared. I watch it head for a stand of daffodil shoots, then I don't see it any more.

As I look into the heart of the blaze, I soon forget the toad. Watching a fire you've started drives everything else out of your mind. It's beautiful and powerful. Nothing can resist it, and it's there because of you. You're its creator. It does what you want it to do.

Like I say, I forget the toad at the time. But that night I have another horrible dream.

I'm watching the fire. The toad crawls out, only this time it's left it too late. Its back end is smoking. The warty skin has begun to melt and trickle down. But worst of all, the poor thing's screaming. Toads don't scream. I know that, even in my dream, but this one's screaming, and it's all my fault. I pick up the smoking toad and look for some water to drop it in. There's a bucket of water just by me, but when I drop it in, the toad breaks in two. The front half falls into the bucket, the back half stays stuck to my hand.

Now *I'm* screaming. I shake and shake my hand again and again. I feel totally sick, but the toad clings to me till I wake up.

I have to switch on my bedside light and look at my hand in the glow before I know for sure it was just a dream. And even then it's ages before I get back to sleep.

Chapter 8
Jackpotty

Two weeks pass. Nothing happens. It says in the paper the police are still investigating the Tesco incident, but they never question Nick. They never come near any of us. Each day I feel more relaxed. Then it's the start of the Easter holidays.

On Monday, Danny calls me. "Normal place," Danny says. "Seven o'clock tonight. Payday." I must be psychic, because I'm just asking myself when I'm going to see the £500 Nick promised.

"That's amazing," I cry. "I was just thinking about that money when –"

Danny cuts in. "Don't babble, Josh. Not on the phone. You never know who might be earwigging. And don't say anything to anyone. See you at seven."

The day drags a bit after that. Well, I've never had £500 at one time. Can't wait to feel those crisp notes on my palm. I saw this cowboy film one time on TV. It was about a bounty hunter. That's someone that goes out and brings the crooks in and gets a reward. It doesn't matter if the crooks come back dead or alive. Anyway, the guy in this film has just brought in a body and got his cash. Someone asks him why he's a bounty hunter and he says, "I'm counting the reasons." Then he smiles and counts the dollar bills in his hand. And that cash was just for shooting a guy, which maybe he enjoyed doing anyway. *I'd* smile if I was him. Like I'll be smiling at seven o'clock when I get *my* cash.

I'm thinking Nick'll be there to pay us, but it's just Danny. He checks up and down the road, then pulls a load of notes out of his backpack. Tens. He lays them on my palm and I flick through them like the bounty hunter, counting. There are fifty tens. I grin.

"Why do we start fires, Danny?" I ask, and before he can answer, I say, "I'm counting the reasons."

Danny shakes his head. "You're crazy, Josh Linfoot. I always said so." He nods towards my money. "Put it in your pocket, take it straight home, hide it. *Not* in your room."

I look at him. "Why not in my room? Where else am I gonna hide it?"

He gives a sigh. "Your mum knows every hiding place in your room, dummy. Trust me. She's checked them out a hundred times for drugs, ciggies, weapons." He smiles. "It's what mums do. Our rooms are private, but only when we're there."

"OK." I nod. "But *where* then?"

"Your dad has a shed, I've seen it." He looks at me. "Find something in there that hasn't been moved for years. Something in a dark corner, with broken stuff all covered in cobwebs. A plant pot or a rusty tin. Shove it in there, only be careful not to break the cobwebs. Don't disturb the dust."

I smile. I've just thought of something. "There's Beth's potty," I tell him. It's the potty she had when she was a baby. I don't know why my mum and dad've kept it, but it's been in the shed for at least four years. It used to be pink, but it's sort of greyish-yellow now, and stuff's fallen on top of it.

Danny nods. "Well there you go. Shove it in the potty, call it your 'jackpotty'." He's witty, Danny. Then he gets serious. "Never have too much money on you. We don't want people asking why we're so rich all of a sudden. That's why Nick paid us in tens, so we won't flash it around."

I do what Danny says. It makes sense. I keep a tenner back, and put the rest in the potty without disturbing anything. £490. It gives me a good feeling, knowing it's there. And I'm really careful with the ten I keep back. Anyway, I'm not one to show off my cash.

I feel rich, but that's not enough. Now I'm not thinking that I might get arrested any day, I need some other excitement. I start wishing Nick would choose something for us to burn.

And there's something else. It's about my sister, Beth. I've always had to listen to my parents going on about how wonderful Beth is, but now it seems all they can talk about is this zoo keeper business. You'd think she'd won the lottery or something. It's Beth this and Beth that. Beth's so sensible. So reliable. So mature. Mature. I mean. She's nine years old. It's doing my head in.

I did say before that I'd started to get a brilliant idea, yeah? Well, this is when I decide to go ahead with it. Looking back, later on, it sounds insane, but at the time it seems OK to me. Clever, even. This is what I'm thinking.

I need excitement.

The most exciting thing is fire.

Nick doesn't seem to be planning a fire anytime soon.

I could plan one myself – there's nothing to it.

My sister's zoo keeper job is doing my head in – it's got to go.

If the school burns, Beth's zoo'll burn too. I get my fire, and her job goes up in smoke. Both problems solved.

Good, eh?

I make my plan. I don't write it down or anything – I'm not stupid. It's all in my head.

I'll work alone, I decide. Even Danny won't know about it. I'll make sure no one sees me – no photo-fit pictures this time. I'll do it on a Saturday when the school's empty. Empty except for those gerbils and guinea pigs. That axolotyl. I'll go straight home after I've done it. That won't be easy – watching's the best bit, but I want Mum to think I've been in my room all the time.

There's this little roof under my window. It's the roof of the kitchen extension. If I hang by my fingers from my sill, my toes just reach it. I've left the house that way loads of times when I've wanted to dodge homework or stuff like that. Getting back up's a bit harder. I have to jump up, hook my fingers on the sill and swing sideways to get one foot on the overflow pipe. But I *can* do it.

The best bit is, we've got a huge tree in the back garden. No nosy neighbours'll see anything.

How hard can it be to commit the perfect crime?

I know what you're thinking – 'What about those poor animals?' Right? Well, what about me? I've been Josh the loser ever since I can remember. Josh the spare part. Josh the waste of space. I've been shoved aside and dumped on, so don't expect me to care about a few rodents and a stupid axolotyl, 'cos I don't. Why should I?

Chapter 9

The Secret of Good Planning

I don't do it in the holidays. I want to get that zoo, and it's not there in school holidays. Kids take the animals home. One of the guinea pigs arrived in Beth's room the day we broke up. It'll be there till she goes back.

Why wait to destroy the zoo? Why don't I settle for just torching the school? Now, later, I really, really wish I had, but it's no use wishing, is it?

So, Easter rolls by. I don't hear anything from Nick and the gang – maybe he doesn't want me involved any more. He knows I wouldn't dare tell anyone about the gang now. The summer term begins. Beth lugs the guinea pig back to school. Kate takes back the axolotyl. The zoo's open for business.

I work on my plan. The big day's going to be the second Saturday of term. On the first Saturday, I spend some time watching the place. I see how old Fallon, the caretaker, potters around, doing stuff in the yard. When he needs to go inside the building, he uses the kitchen door round the back. The main entrance stays locked.

This is a bit of a shame. I was hoping Fallon went in and out the front way. Then I'd be sure he was out of the school before I lobbed my petrol bomb. That's how I'm planning to start the fire. I'm going to fill a bottle full of petrol, cork it with a rag, then set light to the rag and chuck the whole lot into the school.

But I'm not a psycho. I don't want to kill Fallon. I want to be sure he's in his house at the front of the school when I chuck the bomb in. If he's at the front, it's easy. Fallon comes out of the school, goes into his house and in goes the bomb! Then I'm off.

If I chuck the thing in through a side window, it'd make a big noise and Fallon'll come running. I might not have time to get away.

I change my plan. I can't throw the bomb through the kitchen door, because Fallon locks it every time he leaves. I'll have to throw it in through a window right at the back. Fallon will be too far away to hear that, plus it'll be easy for me to escape the back way. I'll watch Fallon cross to his house, then slip round and do the job.

Think of everything – that's the secret of good planning.

I worry about how I'm going to get some petrol. I could go to a petrol station, but people might say, 'What does he want petrol for? What's he going to do with it?' Then I remember. Dad always carries an old red can in the back of the car. It's filled with spare petrol, in case he runs dry in the middle of nowhere.

It's getting dark, Sunday evening. Dad's at the pub, Mum and Beth are watching the telly. So I borrow the car keys from Mum's bag. I take an empty glass bottle from the recycling, unlock the car boot, and fill the bottle up with petrol from the red can. There's still quite a bit of petrol left.

I'm sure no one will notice there's some missing. Then I hide the bottle up the side of the shed.

Easy.

The week drags a bit. I need excitement, and all I get is the same old stuff about Beth the magic zoo keeper. 'Not for much longer,' I keep telling myself, but it feels like forever.

I stop myself from telling Danny. It's not easy, but I've decided to work alone. It's part of my plan. I might tell him after, to boost my cred with the gang. I might. It'll depend how it goes.

On Friday evening I say goodnight to Mum. "I'm really tired. I'm going to have a lie-in tomorrow unless you want me for something. Then I'd better start revising in the afternoon."

I always get up late on Saturday morning, so that's nothing new. But Mum keeps going on at me to revise and she can't believe her luck. She won't mind when I get up as long as I'm planning to revise later.

She says, "Shall I bring a cup of tea up to you in bed?"

I shake my head. "No Mum, thanks. And make sure Beth keeps out of my hair, eh?"

Sheer genius. No one's going to open my door. No one'll know I'll be missing for an hour or so. It's perfect.

I can barely sleep I'm so excited. Saturday is wet and windy. I don't care. In fact it's good. No nosy neighbours in their gardens, so it's even easier for me to get out and back. I can hear Mum and Beth downstairs having breakfast. Dad's gone to the office. Rain rattles on the window, the tree outside sways and ripples in the wind. The phone rings, and I hear Mum tell Beth it's for her. Beth whines and moans on about something, I can't hear what. I don't *want* to hear. She's always moaning about something.

At 9:30 I put on my hoodie, open the window and climb out. It's still raining. There's no one about. I collect the bottle and keep an eye on the window in case Mum looks out. She doesn't. I slip away. The bomb's hidden inside my jacket. In a pocket I have my lighter and a spare, plus a bit of rag to stuff down the bottle's neck.

You have to think of everything.

Chapter 10
The Perfect Crime

It's twenty to ten. I hide behind a wet bush and watch the school. The front doors are locked. No surprise there. "Where's old Fallon?" I mutter to myself. A second later he walks round the side, dangling his keys. He's been round the back. No surprise there, either. You don't want surprises, that's why you plan.

I watch him cross to his house, go inside and close the door. Perfect. I'll be finished quicker than I thought. I break cover, walk across the yard and down the side of the building. There's no rush – he'll be a few minutes at least.

Halfway down I stop, stand the bottle on a windowsill and stuff the rag into the neck. The classroom beyond the window isn't Beth's. Shame. I'd have liked a glimpse of the zoo before it's too late. But still.

I peep round the corner. I knew there wouldn't be anyone there and there isn't. I walk along to the kitchen door and try it. It's locked, of course. Hot on security, old Fallon. I click my lighter and set the rag alight. I quiver with excitement as I watch the tiny flame. "Won't be small for long," I murmur. "Powerful, thanks to me. Destructive. Unstoppable."

I stand back, pick a window and hurl the bomb.

The effect is stunning. The force of my throw shatters window and bottle together. Petrol, flames and oxygen meet in the air with a sound like nothing I've ever heard. Liquid fire drenches the kitchen. The whole place explodes in a sea of leaping flame.

'That was me!' I tell myself. 'I unleashed this power. I'm the boss of it, it's mine.' I laugh out loud, gazing at my work.

For a few seconds I'm totally happy. It's like I'm drunk. For those few seconds I even forget to run. When I *do* leave, I leave laughing.

In a few minutes I'm back in my room. A room I've never left. It's the perfect crime.

"Josh?" Mum raps on my door.

"What's up, Mum?" I yawn.

"Look out of your window. There's smoke. It's near the school. I hope ..."

"Just getting some clothes on," I say. I've been watching the smoke. Enjoying it. I open the door, forcing myself not to grin. "Hope *what*, Mum?"

She hurries to my window. "I hope it isn't the school. Beth's there."

"*Beth?*" Fear stabs me in the gut. "But it's *Saturday*, Mum. Why would she be at school on a ...?"

"Kate rang. They forgot to leave water for the animals yesterday. They're there now. They were going to get the caretaker to let them in. It – it does *seem* to be coming from the school."

I don't want to talk about it. Oh, they got her out. Her and her little friend. But Beth's ear was burned. Her left ear. You might think she got off light, but not if you saw the way she keeps that side of her face turned away in company. Not if you had to watch how she tries to pull her hair over it all the time. I don't think she knows she's doing it.

They never found out who torched the school, killed the animals, and marked Beth for life. Yes, I know – I should've turned myself in and confessed. Easy to say, but terribly hard to do. And Mum and Dad would have been so upset. Mum would blame herself, wonder where she'd gone wrong with me. Dad would never forgive me.

You may think *I* got off light as well, but you're wrong. I have to watch Beth trying to hide her ear. It happens a hundred times a day, and my heart breaks every time, because I love my sister. I never knew I did till Mum said, "Beth's there."

Our books are tested
for children and young people by
children and young people.

Thanks to everyone who consulted on
a manuscript for their time and effort in
helping us to make our books better
for our readers.

About the Author

ROBERT SWINDELLS was born in Bradford in Yorkshire. He wasn't clever at school, but he was good at making up stories and he won his first writing competition at the age of 14.

Robert left school at 15 and had lots of different jobs before he decided to train to be a primary school teacher. After several years of teaching, he became a full time writer.

Robert has a Master's Degree in Peace Studies and was sent to jail for seven days for helping blockade Whitehall as a member of the anti-nuclear movement.

Robert has written 70 books for young people and has won the Carnegie Medal, the Children's Book Award (twice), the Angus Book Award, the Other Award, the Sheffield Children's Book Award, and a number of regional prizes.

He lives with his wife on the Yorkshire moors.

Also by *Robert Swindells* ...

Snapshot

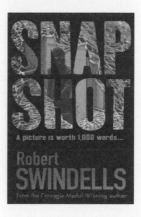

It was my birthday really, but it could have been my deathday. It very nearly was in fact.

Alfie has a great new SLR and he can't wait to try it out. But while he snaps artistic shots of the street outside his home, a gang of robbers smash the window of a jewellery shop and make off with loads of watches and rings.

Alfie's got the whole thing on camera. Now a lot of people want to get their hands on his SLR. And they will stop at nothing ...